THE
OF GLO...

MRS
TITTLE-
MOUSE

Squ... NUTKIN

...NDT...

KT-431-527

TOM
...TTE...

PETERS
...ABBIT...

C130293982

THE TALE
OF
TOM KITTEN

THE TALE OF
TOM KITTEN

BY
BEATRIX POTTER

Author of
"*The Tale of Peter Rabbit*", *&c.*

FREDERICK WARNE

*The reproductions in this book have been made using
the most modern electronic scanning methods from entirely
new transparencies of Beatrix Potter's original watercolours.
They enable Beatrix Potter's skill as an artist to be appreciated
as never before, not even during her own lifetime.*

FREDERICK WARNE

Published by the Penguin Group
27 Wrights Lane, London w8 5tz, England
Viking Penguin Inc., 40 West 23rd Street, New York, New York 10010, USA
Penguin Books Australia Ltd, Ringwood, Victoria, Australia
Penguin Books Canada Ltd, 2801 John Street, Markham, Ontario, Canada l3r 1b4
Penguin Books (NZ) Ltd, 182–190 Wairau Road, Auckland 10, New Zealand

Penguin Books Ltd, Registered Offices: Harmondsworth, Middlesex, England

First published 1907
This edition with new reproductions first published 1987
This impression 1988

Colour reproduction by
East Anglian Engraving Company Ltd, Norwich
Printed and bound in Great Britain by
William Clowes Limited, Beccles and London

0988

DEDICATED

TO ALL

PICKLES,

—ESPECIALLY TO THOSE THAT

GET UPON MY GARDEN WALL

ONCE upon a time there were three little kittens, and their names were Mittens, Tom Kitten, and Moppet.

They had dear little fur coats of their own; and they tumbled about the doorstep and played in the dust.

BUT one day their mother—
Mrs. Tabitha Twitchit—
expected friends to tea; so she
fetched the kittens indoors, to
wash and dress them, before
the fine company arrived.

FIRST she scrubbed their faces (this one is Moppet).

THEN she brushed their fur,
(this one is Mittens).

THEN she combed their tails and whiskers (this is Tom Kitten).

Tom was very naughty, and he scratched.

Mrs. TABITHA dressed Moppet and Mittens in clean pinafores and tuckers; and then she took all sorts of elegant uncomfortable clothes out of a chest of drawers, in order to dress up her son Thomas.

TOM KITTEN was very
fat, and he had grown;
several buttons burst off. His
mother sewed them on again.

WHEN the three kittens were ready, Mrs. Tabitha unwisely turned them out into the garden, to be out of the way while she made hot buttered toast.

"Now keep your frocks clean, children! You must walk on your hind legs. Keep away from the dirty ash-pit, and from Sally Henny Penny, and from the pig-stye and the Puddle-Ducks."

24

MOPPET and Mittens walked down the garden path unsteadily. Presently they trod upon their pinafores and fell on their noses.

When they stood up there were several green smears!

"LET us climb up the rockery, and sit on the garden wall," said Moppet.

They turned their pinafores back to front, and went up with a skip and a jump; Moppet's white tucker fell down into the road.

TOM KITTEN was quite unable to jump when walking upon his hind legs in trousers. He came up the rockery by degrees, breaking the ferns, and shedding buttons right and left.

HE was all in pieces when he reached the top of the wall.

Moppet and Mittens tried to pull him together; his hat fell off, and the rest of his buttons burst.

WHILE they were in diffi-
culties, there was a pit
pat paddle pat! and the three
Puddle-Ducks came along the
hard high road, marching one
behind the other and doing
the goose step—pit pat paddle
pat! pit pat waddle pat!

THEY stopped and stood in a row, and stared up at the kittens. They had very small eyes and looked surprised.

THEN the two duck-birds,
Rebeccah and Jemima
Puddle-Duck, picked up the
hat and tucker and put them
on.

MITTENS laughed so that she fell off the wall. Moppet and Tom descended after her; the pinafores and all the rest of Tom's clothes came off on the way down.

"Come! Mr. Drake Puddle-Duck," said Moppet—"Come and help us to dress him! Come and button up Tom!"

M R. DRAKE PUDDLE-
DUCK advanced in a
slow sideways manner, and
picked up the various articles.

BUT he put them on *himself!* They fitted him even worse than Tom Kitten. "It's a very fine morning!" said Mr. Drake Puddle-Duck.

AND he and Jemima and Rebeccah Puddle-Duck set off up the road, keeping step—pit pat, paddle pat! pit pat, waddle pat!

THEN Tabitha Twitchit
came down the garden
and found her kittens on the
wall with no clothes on.

SHE pulled them off the wall, smacked them, and took them back to the house.

"My friends will arrive in a minute, and you are not fit to be seen; I am affronted," said Mrs. Tabitha Twitchit.

SHE sent them upstairs; and I am sorry to say she told her friends that they were in bed with the measles; which was not true.

QUITE the contrary; they were not in bed: *not* in the least.

Somehow there were very extraordinary noises over-head, which disturbed the dignity and repose of the tea party.

AND I think that some day
I shall have to make
another, larger, book, to tell
you more about Tom Kitten!

AS for the Puddle-Ducks—
they went into a pond.
The clothes all came off
directly, because there were
no buttons.

AND Mr. Drake Puddle-
Duck, and Jemima and
Rebeccah, have been looking
for them ever since.